For Jeanette, George and Iris
– J C

Copyright © 2007 by Good Books, Intercourse, PA 17534
International Standard Book Number: 978-1-56148-592-5

Text and illustrations copyright © Jason Chapman 2007

Original edition published in English by Little Tiger Press,
an imprint of Magi Publications, London, England, 2007.

Printed in Singapore

Library of Congress Cataloging-in-Publication Data
Chapman, Jason.
Ted, Bo and Diz : The First Adventure / Jason Chapman.
p. cm.
Summary: Three friends go to the beach, where they encounter a family of
polar bears and a baby seal, adrift in the ocean on a bed of ice.
ISBN: 978-1-56148-592-5 (hardcover)
[1. Polar Bear--Fiction. 2. Bears--Fiction. 3. Seals--Fiction.
4. Ocean--Fiction. 5. Beaches--Fiction.] I. Title.

PZ7.C368Te 2007
[E]--dc22
2007004508

Ted, Bo and Diz

The First Adventure

Jason Chapman

Good Books

Intercourse, PA 17534
800/762-7171
www.GoodBooks.com

It was a warm, sunny morning.
Ted, Bo and Diz were at the beach.

"It's a lovely day ..." sang Ted as
he pumped up the raft.
"... to be by the ocean!" sang Diz,
shaking out the towels.

"Look," hollered Diz. "Is that an iceberg?"

There, all curled up on the softly rocking bed of ice,
lay a family of polar bears and a baby seal.

One by one, they woke up.

Ted, Bo and Diz paddled gently towards them.
As Bo leaned forward to give the smallest
polar bear a flower, she felt the coolness of
the icy boat on her face.

The little bear had never seen a flower before,
but he knew it was beautiful.

Under the warm sun the bears told stories of their icy world. The new friends played together, making snow castles on their island of ice.

Suddenly there was a dull crack.
The ice beneath Diz's feet broke off
and slipped away.
   "JUMP!" they all shouted.
   Diz jumped high and long, landing
safely with his friends . . .

Their island was melting!
"We could paddle home
in the boat," said
Daddy Polar Bear, but
it was too small for
all of them.

They sat and they
thought. And as they
thought, their
island got smaller . . .

and smaller.

Suddenly Ted jumped
into the boat.
"Wait here!" he said.
"I've got an idea."

"Be careful, Ted!" called Bo.
The new friends huddled together as
they watched Ted paddle far out to sea.

"Ted's coming back," said Mommy Polar Bear.
"He's coming back very fast!" said Diz.
Ted was with a family of whales!
"Hop aboard," said the biggest whale.

Ted, Bo and Diz waved goodbye as the bears and baby seal set off on their long journey home.
Soon the iceberg was no bigger than a pebble on the beach. Bo picked it up and held it until there was nothing left.

"Let's go home," said Ted sadly.
Diz looked out to sea and smiled.

"Look," he said. "Another iceberg!"